D1064666

For Cathy Ballou Mealey,
book buddy and critiquer extraordinaire.
–M. A.

For Henry.
–J. H.

 First published in 2023 by Page Street Kids, an imprint of Page Street Publishing Co., 27 Congress Street, Suite 1511, Salem, MA 01970, www.pagestreetpublishing.com.
 Distributed by Macmillan, sales in Canada by The Canadian Manda Group
ISBN-13: 978-1-64567-712-3. ISBN-10: 1-64567-712-5. CIP data for this book is available from the Library of Congress.
This book was typeset in Adorn Roman. The illustrations were done digitally. Cover and book design by Julia Tyler for Page Street Kids.
Edited by Kayla Tostevin for Page Street Kids. Printed and bound in Shenzhen, Guangdong, China.
23 24 25 26 27 CCO 5 4 3 2 1

Page Street Publishing uses only materials from suppliers who are committed to responsible and sustainable forest management.
Page Street Publishing protects our planet by donating to nonprofits like The Trustees, which focuses on local land conservation.

Pirate & PENGUIN

Mike Allegra
illustrated by Jenn Harney

HOP!

PAGE STREET KIDS

SLIP!
TUMBLE!
TUMBLE!
PLOP!

Ahoy! Avast!
A PARROT?
Shiver me timbers!
This lonely old pirate has been searchin' the Seven Seas for a parrot pal! And what a perfect pirate parrot ye arrrrr!

Though the blazin' sun seems ta have faded yer parroty plumage. . . .

THAR YE ARRRRRR! Yer the prettiest pirate parrot I's ever seen!
Now set yerself on me stout shoulder like a good pirate's parrot should.

GAH!

OOCH!

UGH!

ARRRR! ME UNDERGARRRRRMENTS!

Methinks
we be makin' ye a
ground parrot.

Can ye talk?
Say "Ahoy, mateys."
Ahoy, mateys!
AHOY, MATEYS! AHOY, MATEYS!!
Hm.
Maybe ye prefer ta say other words. . . .
Thar she blows?

Batten down the hatches?
Mizzenmast?
Landlubber?
Hornswoggle?
Doubloons?
Booty?
TALK,
PARROT! TALK!

HO

OOONK!

Well, "honk" be a word, I suppose.
Maybe ye be an able seaman. I can feel the wind a-turning on me ruddy cheeks! Trim sail on the mizzenmast, Parrot, and haul wind!
YOINK!

An able first try.
Have a cracker.

HUH-HWAAK
PTOOI!

SNOGGERS!

'Tis be the last straw!
I give ye me last crumb o' food
and ye expectorate on me freshly swabbed poop deck!
'TIS MUTINY!
INSUBORDINATION!
SUBPARRRRRR TABLE MANNERS!

You be the worst
good-fer-nothing parrot
I'S EVER SEEN!

Hey, Parrot. Where ye goin'?
WAIT!
Don't walk the plank!
Come back!
NOOOOO

O!

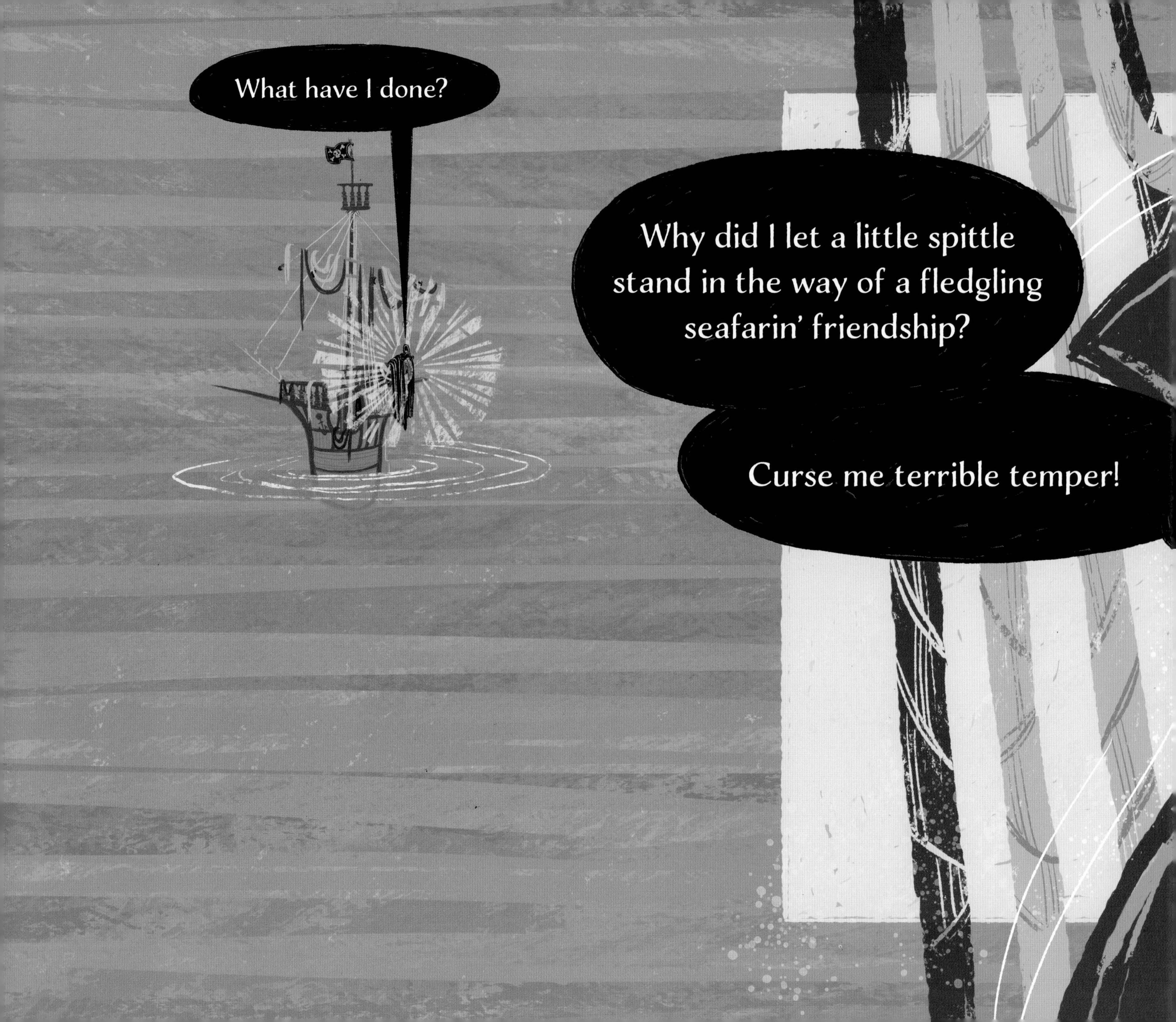
What have I done?
Why did I let a little spittle stand in the way of a fledgling seafarin' friendship?
Curse me terrible temper!

I be a rotting rapscallion!
A scurvy scallywag!
A pirate-y poopie head!
Forgive me, Parrot!
PLEASE FORGIVE *MEEEEEE!*

HONK
Me parrot!
ME FRIEND!

Me fish?

You, me hearty,
be the strangest parrot I's ever seen.

But I like ye
just the way ye arrrrrrr!